To Cosmo, Pickle, and Princess Cupcake,
my favorite hounds. - B.D.

For Manon, thanks for letting me sleep
so well to illustrate this book! - C.A.

tiger tales
5 River Road, Suite 128, Wilton, CT 06897
Published in the United States 2017
Originally published in Great Britain 2017 by Little Tiger Press
Text by Becky Davies
Text copyright © 2017 Little Tiger Press
Illustrations copyright © 2017 Caroline Attia
Photographs used under license from Shutterstock.com
ISBN-13: 978-1-68010-043-3
ISBN-10: 1-68010-043-2
Printed in China
LTP/1400/1676/1016

For more insight and activities, visit us at
www.tigertalesbooks.com

The Three Little PUGS and the Big, Bad CAT

by Becky Davies

Illustrated by Caroline Attia

tiger tales

Once upon a time, there were three little pugs named Bubbles, Bandit, and Beauty. They lived with their mother in a tiny kennel in the woods.

"You're not puppies anymore," said Mother Pug. "It's time you left to build houses of your own."

What kind of houses should we build?

Take these snacks and watch out for the **Big, Bad Cat**. She's the meanest feline around and will do anything for food. Build strong houses to keep that clever kitty out.

So off the three little pugs went, their backpacks bulging with biscuits.

Bandit and Beauty bounded ahead, while Bubbles dragged his paws at the back.

"I'm starving!"

he wailed, plopping himself down on the ground.
"Can't I eat just a *couple* of treats?"
"You have to build a house first. Remember the Big, Bad Cat!" warned Beauty.

Come back here, tail!

"Fine," said Bubbles, looking around. "Then I'll build my house right here out of . . . this straw." And that's exactly what he did.

As soon as Bubbles had finished building his straw house, he turned greedily to his food, licking his little puggy lips.

He opened his mouth as **wide** as it would go, but before he could take a bite, he heard a noise outside.

"**Humph!** Can't a pug enjoy his meal in peace?" snorted Bubbles, and he waddled over to the window to take a look.

"Then I'll huff, and I'll puff, and I'll blow your house down!"

cried the cat, pulling out a hairdryer,

"and I'll barely have to lift a paw."

Oh, no!
It was the Big, Bad Cat!
"Little pug, little pug, let me come in!" yowled the Big, Bad Cat.
"N . . . not by the hairs on my chinny chin chin!" trembled Bubbles, scrambling to cover his food dish.

The hairdryer whirred ... and it whooshed ... and it BLEW THE HOUSE DOWN!

"Yikes!" yelped Bubbles, and he scurried away as fast as he could.

But Bandit wouldn't listen. He ran around happily, chewing sticks, digging holes, and building himself a messy little stick house.

Bandit had just said good-bye to Beauty and was about to gobble up his first dog biscuit when Bubbles hurtled through his front door, wheezing. "The Big, Bad Cat . . ." panted Bubbles. "Coming . . . this way . . . protect the treats!"

But just then, a giant shadow fell across the window. Huddled together, the pugs looked out to see . . .

Sharp, scratchy claws, a terrible twitching tail, and mean beady eyes.

"Little pugs, little pugs, let me come in!" howled the Big, Bad Cat.

"N . . . not by the hairs on our chinny chin chins!" trembled Bubbles and Bandit.

"Then I'll huff, and I'll puff, and I'll blow your house down!" the cat declared, pulling out a leaf blower and aiming it at the house of sticks. "And I won't even ruffle my fur," she purred.

The leaf blower spat . . . and it sputtered

Help! My sticks!

Bandit

Deep in the forest, Beauty had walked and walked until at last she found a pile of bricks. She knew exactly how she'd build her house . . . .

Just as the last brick was laid, Bandit and Bubbles came bursting through the trees.

"Beauty! Beauty! The **Big, Bad Cat** is coming!" panted Bandit. "She ate our food!" wailed Bubbles. "We're all going to starve!"

"Don't worry; everything is under control," said Beauty as she gathered her brothers into a huddle. "It's time for plan B, boys! Now listen carefully . . . ."

TOP SECRET PLAN 'B

When the **Big, Bad Cat** reached the brick house, all was quiet. Too quiet.

"Little pugs, little pugs, let me come in!" growled the cat.

But there was no response.

She peeked inside to see . . .

. . . a **bulging** backpack and three pug-shaped lumps on the couch.

"It's no use hiding," the Big, Bad Cat purred smugly. "I'll still huff, and I'll puff, and I'll blow your house down! And I won't even tangle a whisker." She pulled out a giant fan and pointed it at the brick house.

The fan blustered . . . and it blasted . . .

but the house stood strong. This would call for something more powerful . . .

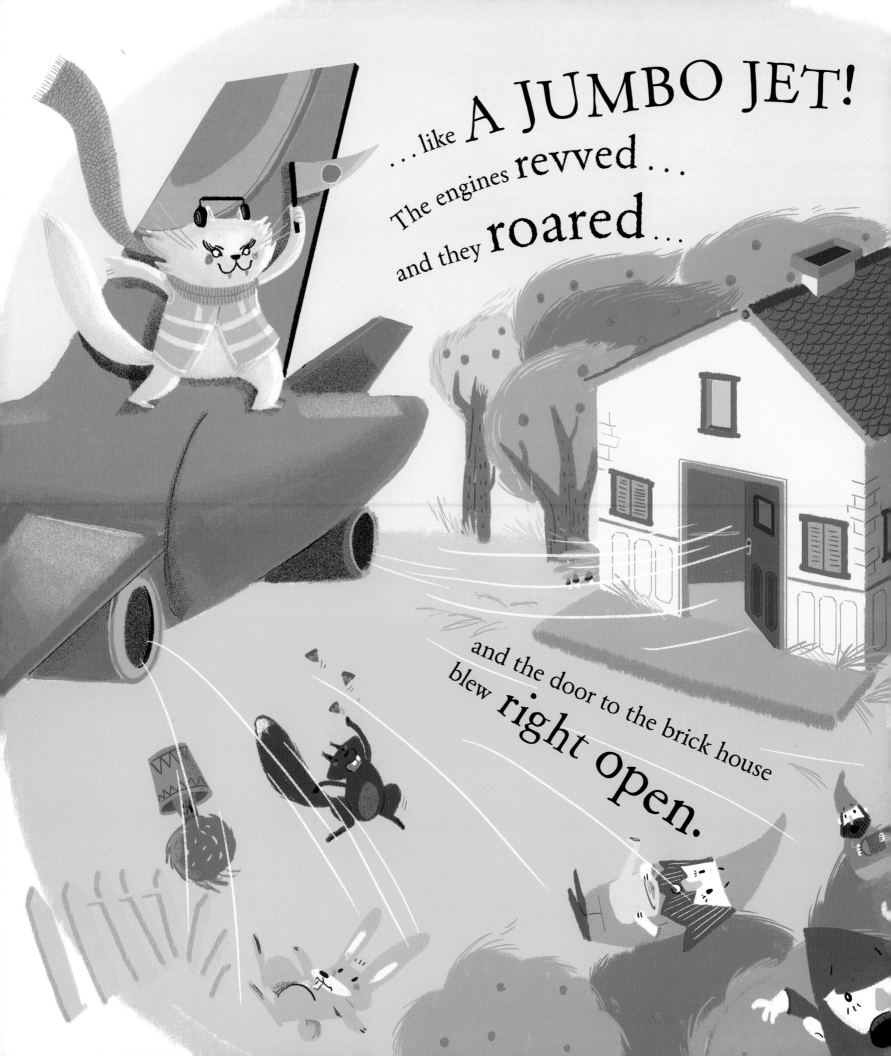

The Big, Bad Cat strutted inside, victorious.

But the backpack was full of sticks! And the lumps on the couch were nothing but cushions!

The Big, Bad Cat was FURIOUS. She yowled and she howled, she hissed and she spat, her eyes narrowed, her tail twitched, and she stamped her paws until . . .

"Muffin!" trilled a voice through the trees.

"Oh, MUFFIN! Time for din-din!"

Muffin

With a flick of her tail, the cat trotted back home through the woods, discarding her disguises.

"There you are, my itty bitty MUFFIN PIE!"
said Mrs. Honeybun, scooping her up.

"I have the most wonderful surprise for my PRETTY-WITTY
MUFFY-WUFFY. Come with me, PRINCESS."
And she carried her inside the house.

Muffin

And the three little pugs and the Big, Bad Cat lived
happily ever after ... well, almost!